AF575802

CONTINENTAL GT
BY BENTLEY

A Crabtree Branches Book

Tracy Nelson Maurer

School-to-Home Support for Caregivers and Teachers

This high-interest book is designed to motivate striving students with engaging topics while building fluency, vocabulary, and an interest in reading. Here are a few questions and activities to help the reader build upon his or her comprehension skills.

Before Reading:

- *What do I think this book is about?*
- *What do I know about this topic?*
- *What do I want to learn about this topic?*
- *Why am I reading this book?*

During Reading:

- *I wonder why...*
- *I'm curious to know...*
- *How is this like something I already know?*
- *What have I learned so far?*

After Reading:

- *What was the author trying to teach me?*
- *What are some details?*
- *How did the photographs and captions help me understand more?*
- *Read the book again and look for the vocabulary words.*
- *What questions do I still have?*

Extension Activities:

- *What was your favorite part of the book? Write a paragraph on it.*
- *Draw a picture of your favorite thing you learned from the book.*

TABLE OF CONTENTS

HELLO, CONTI!

Walter Owen (W.O.) Bentley started his car company in 1919. His goal was "to build a good car, a fast car, the best in its class." His company did just that for decades before Bentley fans welcomed the modern Continental GT in 2003. This athletic two-door luxury car quickly became a favorite of celebrities, royals, and **elite** drivers around the world.

"Conti" is the nickname for the Continental GT. The "GT" stands for grand touring—high-speed power and luxury for long drives.

The Continental GT price starts around $200,000.

Bentley makes Continental GTs in hardtop **coupes** and convertible body styles. The Continental GT Mulliner is a super-luxury car. It comes in a hardtop or convertible. Owners can customize nearly *everything*.

Robert Downey Jr., Paris Hilton, Jennifer Lopez, and Ludacris are all Conti owners.

POWERFUL PROWLER

The Continental GT prowls the highways with one of two powerful engines. Both motors reach top speeds of about 200 mph (321 km/h).

The V8 motor positions eight **cylinders** in a V shape. This motor can pounce from 0 to 60 mph (100 km/h) in 4.0 seconds.

The more expensive W12 engine positions twelve cylinders in a W shape. With this motor, the Conti surges from 0 to 60 mph (97 km/h) in 3.7 seconds.

It takes 45 people six and a half hours to build one W12 engine.

Continental GTs use an all-wheel drive system to grip the road at high speeds or in poor weather. Another system handles each **axle** to add control and smooth the bumps.

V8
C1 BML

ART ON WHEELS

Bentley designers have sculpted the Conti like a masterpiece. The sleek shape flows from the nose toward the haunches above the back wheels. At the rear, four oval **exhaust** pipes echo the taillight shape.

Look for Bentley's black "B" badges on the hood, trunk, wheels, and steering wheel. The self-leveling "B" badges stay upright on the wheels even while they are spinning. Bentley engineers think of everything!

Bentley Motors builds its cars in Crewe, England. British people say "bonnet" for hood and "boot" for trunk. They also drive on the left side of the road, so the Continental GT steering wheel is on the right side of the car there.

FIRST-CLASS CABIN

The Continental GT cockpit features a first-class interior. Its center dashboard shows the outside temperature, time, and compass on stunning old-school **analog** gauges. This center panel can be flipped over to reveal a 12.3 inch (31.2 cm) digital infotainment display.

Double-diamond quilted seats plump up the comfort.

Conti's 2+2 seating means that two adults fit comfortably in the front seats and two more people can squeeze into the back. The trunk holds five carry-on suitcases, so at least everyone can pack a bag for the weekend.

A heated steering wheel is just one of the Conti's many luxury touches.

The Continental GT Mulliner shifts the luxury one step up. **Bespoke**, or custom, options make each car unique to the owner. Bentley's experts craft many of the details by hand.

Until the 1940s, cloth was considered more elegant than leather interiors. Bespoke Mulliners and other Bentleys built for the British Royal Family may still use rich cloth interiors.

DRIVING HELP

The Continental GT offers many options for easier and safer driving. For example, **adaptive** cruise control adjusts the Conti's speed to keep a safe distance from the car ahead. Another system can sense if someone walks in front of the car when the vehicle is moving—and instantly hits the brakes.

Drive
11:42
Night vision
Head-up display
Intelligent coasting
Raise suspension
Blind spot assist
Bentley Safeguard
SCREEN
PHONE
OK
BENTLEY
071M647
MANUFACTURER

A night vision option helps Conti drivers see the road after dark. The Continental GT also has beautiful **LED** headlights and taillights. The lights seem to sparkle like diamonds with a design inspired by fine cut crystal glass.

The Conti welcomes passengers with an option that slowly brightens the lights as the driver approaches.

QUALITY BEYOND QUALITY

Every Bentley vehicle passes more than 500 checklist items before it rolls out the door. Quality matters at every step, not just at the end of production.

A wood specialist checks every inch (cm) of the raw wood before it even comes to the plant—a step that takes two days.

All the wood used in an entire car comes from the exact same tree to make sure the pattern and color stay the same over time.

More than 4,000 people work at the Bentley Motors factory in England. They build about 10,000 cars each year there. It takes more than 530 people around 110 hours to build one Continental GT.

When the COVID-19 pandemic happened, the Bentley factory used its 3D technology to make more than 30,000 face shields for local health centers and care homes.

THINKING AHEAD

Bentley Motors launched into its next 100 years with a passion for protecting the planet. Already, the factory uses 20,815 solar panels to supply up to 40 percent of the site's electricity—enough to power 1,200 houses for a year.

Rolls-Royce bought Bentley Motors in 1931. The Volkswagon Group purchased the company in 1998. All along, the focus has been to build the best car in its class. So far, so good.

GLOSSARY

adaptive (uh-DAP-tiv): Able to adapt, or change to suit particular circumstances

analog (an-UH-lawg): Using moving parts to measure

axle (AK-suhl): The rod that wheels spin around

bespoke (bee-SPOKE): Made specifically for one person or customer

coupés (coo-PAYS in Europe; COOPS in the U.S.): Two-seat cars with sloping rooflines

cylinders (SIL-uhn-durz): Tube-shaped chambers in an engine

elite (i-LEET or AY-leet): Describes very rich or important people

exhaust (ig-ZAWST): Waste gas or steam released by an engine

LED (EL-EE-DEE): Stands for "light-emitting diode," a type of light source

INDEX

WEBSITES TO VISIT

https://www.bentleymotors.com

https://www.topgear.com/car-reviews/bentley/continental-gt

https://www.caranddriver.com/bentley/continental-gt

ABOUT THE AUTHOR

Tracy Nelson Maurer

Tracy Nelson Maurer has written more than 100 nonfiction books for young readers. She lives in Minnesota where she happily drives a minivan.

We recognize that some words, model names, and designations, for example, mentioned herein are the property of the trademark holder. We use them for identification purposes only. This is not an official publication.

Produced by: Blue Door Education for Crabtree Publishing
Written by: Tracy Nelson Maurer
Designed by: Jennifer Dydyk
Edited by: Kelli Hicks
Proofreader: Janine Deschenes

Photographs: Cover: Logo graphic © Shutterstock.com/officeku, speedometer © Shutterstock.com/Panuwatccn, shiny car hood top left © Shutterstock.com/ Inked Pixels, Bentley photo © Bentley Motors Limited. All rights reserved, Title page: © Bentley Motors Limited. All rights reserved, PG 4: © Dmitry Eagle Orlov / Shutterstock.com, PG 5: ©Tinseltown / Shutterstock.com, DFree / Shutterstock.com, Tinseltown / Shutterstock.com, Featureflash Photo Agency / Shutterstock.com, PG 6: Featureflash Photo Agency / Shutterstock.com, PG 7: KULLAPONG PARCHERAT / Shutterstock.com, PG 8-9: ©Bentley Motors Limited. All rights reserved (all), PG 10-11: ©Bentley Motors Limited. All rights reserved (all), PG 12: ©Bentley Motors Limited. All rights reserved, PG 13: ©Bentley Motors Limited. All rights reserved, ©Steve Mann / Shutterstock.com (top), PG 14-15: ©Bentley Motors Limited. All rights reserved (all), PG 16-17: ©Bentley Motors Limited. All rights reserved (all), PG 18-19: ©Bentley Motors Limited. All rights reserved (all), PG 20-21: ©Bentley Motors Limited. All rights reserved (all), PG 22-23: ©Bentley Motors Limited. All rights reserved (all), PG 24-25: ©Bentley Motors Limited. All rights reserved (all), PG 26-27: ©Bentley Motors Limited. All rights reserved (all), PG 28-29: ©Bentley Motors Limited. All rights reserved (all). Special thanks to the Bentley Motor Company for contributing images to help build literacy and company car awareness for children through nonfiction/editorial texts.

Library and Archives Canada Cataloguing in Publication

Title: Continental GT by Bentley / Tracy Nelson Maurer.
Names: Maurer, Tracy Nelson, 1965- author.
Description: Series statement: Luxury rides | "A Crabtree branches book". | Includes index.
Identifiers: Canadiana (print) 20210220546 | Canadiana (ebook) 20210220554 | ISBN 9781427154828 (hardcover) | ISBN 9781427154880 (softcover) | ISBN 9781427154941 (HTML) | ISBN 9781427155009 (EPUB) | ISBN 9781427155061 (read-along ebook)
Subjects: LCSH: Bentley automobile—Juvenile literature.
Classification: LCC TL215.B4 M38 2022 | DDC j629.222/2—dc23

Library of Congress Cataloging-in-Publication Data

Names: Maurer, Tracy Nelson, 1965- author.
Title: Continental GT by Bentley / Tracy Nelson Maurer.
Description: New York : Crabtree Publishing Company, [2022] | Series: Luxury rides | Includes index.
Identifiers: LCCN 2021022087 (print) | LCCN 2021022088 (ebook) | ISBN 9781427154828 (hardcover) | ISBN 9781427154880 (paperback) | ISBN 9781427154941 (ebook) | ISBN 9781427155009 (epub) | ISBN 9781427155061
Subjects: LCSH: Bentley automobile--Juvenile literature. | Sports cars--Juvenile literature.
Classification: LCC TL215.B4 M38 2022 (print) | LCC TL215.B4 (ebook) | DDC 629.222/2--dc23
LC record available at https://lccn.loc.gov/2021022087

LC ebook record available at https://lccn.loc.gov/2021022088

Crabtree Publishing Company

www.crabtreebooks.com 1-800-387-7650

Copyright © 2022 **CRABTREE PUBLISHING COMPANY**

All rights reserved. No part of this publication may be reproduced, stored in a retrieval system or be transmitted in any form or by any means, electronic, mechanical, photocopying, recording, or otherwise, without the prior written permission of Crabtree Publishing Company. In Canada: We acknowledge the financial support of the Government of Canada through the Canada Book Fund for our publishing activities.

Published in the United States
Crabtree Publishing
347 Fifth Avenue, Suite 1402-145
New York, NY, 10016

Published in Canada
Crabtree Publishing
616 Welland Ave.
St. Catharines, ON, L2M 5V6